THE FEATHER PILLOW

by

HORACIO QUIROGA

The Feather Pillow

Alicia's entire honeymoon gave her hot and cold shivers. A blonde, angelic, and timid young girl, the childish fancies she had dreamed about being a bride had been chilled by her husband's rough character. She loved him very much, nonetheless, although sometimes she gave a light shudder when, as they returned home through the streets together at night, she cast a furtive glance at the impressive stature of her Jordan, who had been silent for an hour. He, for his part, loved her profoundly but never let it be seen.

For three months--they had been married in April--they lived in a special kind of bliss.

Doubtless she would have wished less severity in the rigorous sky of love, more expansive and less cautious tenderness, but her husband's impassive manner always restrained her.

The house in which they lived influenced her chills and shuddering to no small degree. The whiteness of the silent patio--friezes, columns, and marble statues--produced the wintry impression of an enchanted palace. Inside the glacial brilliance of stucco, the completely bare walls, affirmed the sensation of unpleasant coldness. As one crossed from one room to another, the echo of his steps reverberated throughout the house, as if long abandonment had sensitized its resonance.

Alicia passed the autumn in this strange love nest. She had determined, however, to cast a veil over her former dreams and live like a sleeping beauty in the hostile house, trying not to think about anything until her husband arrived each evening.

It is not strange that she grew thin. She had a light attack of influenza that dragged on insidiously for days and days: after that Alicia's health never returned. Finally one afternoon she was able to go into the garden, supported on her husband's arm. She looked around listlessly.

Suddenly Jordan, with deep tenderness, ran his hand very slowly over her head, and Alicia instantly burst into sobs, throwing her arms around his neck. For a long time she cried out all the fears she had kept silent, redoubling her weeping at Jordan's slightest caress. Then her sobs subsided, and she stood a long while, her face hidden in the hollow of his neck, not moving or speaking a word.

This was the last day Alicia was well enough to be up. On the following day she awakened feeling faint. Jordan's doctor examined her with minute attention, prescribing calm and absolute rest.

'I don't know,' he said to Jordan at the street door. 'She has a great weakness that I am unable to explain. And with no vomiting, nothing...if she wakes tomorrow as she did today, call me at once.

When she awakened the following day, Alicia was worse. There was a consultation. It was agreed there was an anaemia of incredible progression, completely inexplicable. Alicia had no more fainting spells, but she was visibly moving toward death. The lights were lighted all day long in her bedroom, and there was complete silence. Hours went by without the slightest sound.

Alicia dozed. Jordan virtually lived in the drawing room, which was also always lighted. With tireless persistence he paced ceaselessly from one end of the room to the other. The carpet swallowed his steps. At times he entered the bedroom and continued his silent pacing back and forth alongside the bed, stopping for an instant at each end to regard his wife.

Suddenly Alicia began to have hallucinations, vague images, at first seeming to float in the air, then descending to floor level. Her eyes excessively wide, she stared continuously at the carpet on either side of the head of her bed. One night she suddenly focused on one spot. Then she opened her mouth to scream, and pearls of sweat suddenly beaded her nose and lips.

'Jordan! Jordan!' she clamoured, rigid with fright, still staring at the carpet.

Jordan ran to the bedroom, and, when she saw him appear, Alicia screamed with terror.

'It's I, Alicia, it's I!'

Alicia looked at him confusedly; she looked at the carpet; she looked at him once again; and after a long moment of stupefied confrontation, she regained her senses. She smiled and took her husband's hand in hers, caressing it, trembling, for half an hour.

Among her most persistent hallucinations was that of an anthropoid poised on his fingertips on the carpet, staring at her.

The doctors returned, but to no avail. They saw before them a diminishing life, a life bleeding away day by day, hour by hour, absolutely without their knowing why. During their last consultation Alicia lay in a stupor while they took her pulse, passing her inert wrist from one to another. They observed her a long time in silence and then moved into the dining room.

'Phew. . .' The discouraged chief physician shrugged his shoulders. 'It is an inexplicable case.

There is little we can do. . .'

'That's my last hope!' Jordan groaned. And he staggered blindly against the table.

Alicia's life was fading away in the subdelirium of anaemia, a delirium which grew worse through the evening hours but which let up somewhat after dawn. The illness never worsened during the daytime, but each morning she awakened pale as death, almost in a swoon. It seemed only at night that her life drained out of her in new waves of blood. Always when she awakened she had the sensation of lying collapsed in the bed with a million-pound weight on top of her.

Following the third day of this relapse she never left her bed again. She could scarcely move her head.

She did not want her bed to be touched, not even to have her bedcovers arranged. Her crepuscular terrors advanced now in the form of monsters that dragged themselves toward the bed and laboriously climbed upon the bedspread.

Then she lost consciousness. The final two days she raved ceaselessly in a weak voice. The lights funereally illuminated the bedroom and drawing room. In the deathly silence of the house the only sound was the monotonous delirium from the bedroom and the dull echoes of Jordan's eternal pacing.

Finally, Alicia died. The servant, when she came in afterward to strip the now empty bed, stared wonderingly for a moment at the pillow.

'Sir!' she called Jordan in a low voice. 'There are stains on the pillow that look like blood.'

Jordan approached rapidly and bent over the pillow. Truly, on the case, on both sides of the hollow left by Alicia's head, were two small dark spots.

'They look like punctures,' the servant murmured after a moment of motionless observation.

'Hold it up to the light,' Jordan told her.

The servant raised the pillow but immediately dropped it and stood staring at it, livid and trembling. Without knowing why, Jordan felt the hair rise on the back of his neck.

'What is it?' he murmured in a hoarse voice.

'It's very heavy,' the servant whispered, still trembling.

Jordan picked it up; it was extraordinarily heavy. He carried it out of the room, and on the dining room table he ripped open the case and the ticking with a slash. The top feathers floated away, and the servant, her mouth opened wide, gave a scream of horror and covered her face with her clenched fists: in the bottom of the pillowcase, among the feathers, slowly moving its hairy legs, was a monstrous animal, a living, viscous ball. It was so swollen one could scarcely make out its mouth.

Night after night, since Alicia had taken to her bed, this abomination had stealthily applied its mouth-- its proboscis one might better say--to the girl's temples, sucking her blood. The puncture was scarcely perceptible. The daily plumping of the pillow had doubtlessly at first impeded its progress, but as soon as the girl could no longer move, the suction became vertiginous. In five days, in five nights, the monster had drained Alicia's life away.

These parasites of feathered creatures, diminutive in their hatitual environment, reach enormous proportions under certain conditions. Human blood seems particularly favourable to them, and it is not rare to encounter them in feather pillows.

THE END

THE PERMANENT
STILETTO

by

W. C. MORROW

The Permanent Stiletto

I had sent in all haste for Dr. Rowell, but as yet he had not arrived, and the strain was terrible. There lay my young friend upon his bed in the hotel, and I believed that he was dying. Only the jewelled handle of the knife was visible at his breast; the blade was wholly sheathed in his body.

"Pull it out, old fellow," begged the sufferer through white, drawn lips, his gasping voice being hardly less distressing than the unearthly look in his eyes.

"No, Arnold," said I, as I held his hand and gently stroked his forehead. It may have been instinct, it may have been a certain knowledge of anatomy that made me refuse.

"Why not? It hurts," he gasped. It was pitiful to see him suffer, this strong, healthy, daring, reckless young fellow.

Dr. Rowell walked in—a tall, grave man, with gray hair. He went to the bed and I pointed to the knife-handle, with its great, bold ruby in the end and its diamonds and emeralds alternating in quaint designs in the sides. The physician started. He felt Arnold's pulse and looked puzzled.

"When was this done?" he asked.

"About twenty minutes ago," I answered.

The physician started out, beckoning me to follow.

"Stop!" said Arnold. We obeyed. "Do you wish to speak of me?" he asked.

"Yes," replied the physician, hesitating.

"Speak in my presence then," said my friend; "I fear nothing." It was said in his old, imperious way, although his suffering must have been great.

"If you insist——"

"I do."

"Then," said the physician, "if you have any matters to adjust they should be attended to at once. I can do nothing for you."

"How long can I live?" asked Arnold.

The physician thoughtfully stroked his gray beard. "It depends," he finally said; "if the knife be withdrawn you may live three minutes; if it be allowed to remain you may possibly live an hour or two—not longer."

Arnold never flinched.

"Thank you," he said, smiling faintly through his pain; "my friend here will pay you. I have some things to do. Let the knife remain." He turned his eyes to mine, and, pressing my hand, said, affectionately, "And I thank you, too, old fellow, for not pulling it out."

The physician, moved by a sense of delicacy, left the room, saying, "Ring if there is a change. I will be in the hotel office." He had not gone far when he turned and came back. "Pardon me," said he, "but there is a young surgeon in the hotel who is said to be a very skilful man. My specialty is not surgery, but medicine. May I call him?"

"Yes," said I, eagerly; but Arnold smiled and shook his head. "I fear there will not be time," he said. But I refused to heed him and directed that the surgeon be called immediately. I was writing at Arnold's dictation when the two men entered the room.

There was something of nerve and assurance in the young surgeon that struck my attention. His manner, though quiet, was bold and straightforward and his movements sure and quick. This young man had already distinguished himself in the performance of some difficult hospital laparotomies, and he was at that sanguine age when ambition looks through the spectacles of experiment. Dr. Raoul Entrefort was the new-comer's name. He was a Creole, small and dark, and he had travelled and studied in Europe.

"Speak freely," gasped Arnold, after Dr. Entrefort had made an examination.

"What think you, doctor?" asked Entrefort of the older man.

"I think," was the reply, "that the knife-blade has penetrated the ascending aorta, about two inches above the heart. So long as the blade remains in the wound the escape of blood is comparatively small, though certain; were the blade withdrawn the heart would almost instantly empty itself through the aortal wound."

Meanwhile, Entrefort was deftly cutting away the white shirt and the undershirt, and soon had the breast exposed. He examined the gem-studded hilt with the keenest interest.

"You are proceeding on the assumption, doctor," he said, "that this weapon is a knife."

"Certainly," answered Dr. Rowell, smiling; "what else can it be?"

"It *is* a knife," faintly interposed Arnold.

"Did you see the blade?" Entrefort asked him, quickly.

"I did—for a moment."

Entrefort shot a quick look at Dr. Rowell and whispered, "Then it is *not* suicide." Dr. Rowell looked puzzled and said nothing.

"I must disagree with you, gentlemen," quietly remarked Entrefort; "this is not a knife." He examined the

6

handle very narrowly. Not only was the blade entirely concealed from view within Arnold's body, but the blow had been so strongly delivered that the skin was depressed by the guard. "The fact that it is not a knife presents a very curious series of facts and contingencies," pursued Entrefort, with amazing coolness, "some of which are, so far as I am informed, entirely novel in the history of surgery."

A quizzical expression, faintly amused and manifestly interested, was upon Dr. Rowell's face. "What is the weapon, doctor?" he asked.

"A stiletto."

Arnold started. Dr. Rowell appeared confused. "I must confess," he said, "my ignorance of the differences among these penetrating weapons, whether dirks, daggers, stilettos, poniards, or bowie-knives."

"With the exception of the stiletto," explained Entrefort, "all the weapons you mention have one or two edges, so that in penetrating they cut their way. A stiletto is round, is ordinarily about half an inch or less in diameter at the guard, and tapers to a sharp point. It penetrates solely by pushing the tissues aside in all directions. You will understand the importance of that point."

Dr. Rowell nodded, more deeply interested than ever.

"How do you know it is a stiletto, Dr. Entrefort?" I asked.

"The cutting of these stones is the work of Italian lapidaries," he said, "and they were set in Genoa. Notice, too, the guard. It is much broader and shorter than the guard of an edged weapon; in fact, it is nearly round. This weapon is about four hundred years old, and would be cheap at twenty thousand florins. Observe, also, the darkening color of your friend's breast in the immediate vicinity of the guard; this indicates that the tissues have been bruised by the crowding of the 'blade,' if I may use the term."

"What has all this to do with me?" asked the dying man.

"Perhaps a great deal, perhaps nothing. It brings a single ray of hope into your desperate condition."

Arnold's eyes sparkled and he caught his breath. A tremor passed all through him, and I felt it in the hand I was holding. Life was sweet to him, then, after all— sweet to this wild dare-devil who had just faced death with such calmness! Dr. Rowell, though showing no sign of jealousy, could not conceal a look of incredulity.

"With your permission," said Entrefort, addressing Arnold, "I will do what I can to save your life."

"You may," said the poor boy.

"But I shall have to hurt you."

"Well."

"Perhaps very much."

"Well."

"And even if I succeed (the chance is one in a thousand) you will never be a sound man, and a constant and terrible danger will always be present."

"Well."

Entrefort wrote a note and sent it away in haste by a bell-boy.

"Meanwhile," he resumed, "your life is in imminent danger from shock, and the end may come in a few minutes or hours from that cause. Attend without delay to whatever matters may require settling, and Dr. Rowell," glancing at that gentleman, "will give you something to brace you up. I speak frankly, for I see that you are a man of extraordinary nerve. Am I right?"

"Be perfectly candid," said Arnold.

Dr. Rowell, evidently bewildered by his cyclonic young associate, wrote a prescription, which I sent by a boy to be filled. With unwise zeal I asked Entrefort,—

"Is there not danger of lockjaw?"

"No," he replied; "there is not a sufficiently extensive injury to peripheral nerves to induce traumatic tetanus."

I subsided. Dr. Rowell's medicine came and I administered a dose. The physician and the surgeon then retired. The poor sufferer straightened up his business. When it was done he asked me,—

"What is that crazy Frenchman going to do to me?"

"I have no idea; be patient."

In less than an hour they returned, bringing with them a keen-eyed, tall young man, who had a number of tools wrapped in an apron. Evidently he was unused to such scenes, for he became deathly pale upon seeing the ghastly spectacle on my bed. With staring eyes and open mouth he began to retreat towards the door, stammering,—

"I—I can't do it."

"Nonsense, Hippolyte! Don't be a baby. Why, man, it is a case of life and death!"

"But—look at his eyes! he is dying!"

Arnold smiled. "I am not dead, though," he gasped.

"I—I beg your pardon," said Hippolyte.

Dr. Entrefort gave the nervous man a drink of brandy and then said,—

"No more nonsense, my boy; it must be done. Gentlemen, allow me to introduce Mr. Hippolyte, one of the most original, ingenious, and skilful machinists in the country."

Hippolyte, being modest, blushed as he bowed. In order to conceal his confusion he unrolled his apron on the table with considerable noise of rattling tools.

"I have to make some preparations before you may begin, Hippolyte, and I want you to observe me that you may become used not only to the sight of fresh blood, but also, what is more trying, the odor of it."

Hippolyte shivered. Entrefort opened a case of surgical instruments.

"Now, doctor, the chloroform," he said, to Dr. Rowell.

"I will not take it," promptly interposed the sufferer; "I want to know when I die."

"Very well," said Entrefort; "but you have little nerve now to spare. We may try it without chloroform, however. It will be better if you can do without. Try your best to lie still while I cut."

"What are you going to do?" asked Arnold.

"Save your life, if possible."

"How? Tell me all about it."

"Must you know?"

"Yes."

"Very well, then. The point of the stiletto has passed entirely through the aorta, which is the great vessel rising out of the heart and carrying the aerated blood to the arteries. If I should withdraw the weapon the blood would rush from the two holes in the aorta and you would soon be dead. If the weapon had been a knife, the parted tissue would have yielded, and the blood would have been forced out on either side of the blade and would have caused death. As it is, not a drop of blood has escaped from the aorta into the thoracic cavity. All that is left for us to do, then, is to allow the stiletto to remain permanently in the aorta. Many difficulties at once present themselves, and I do not wonder at Dr. Rowell's look of surprise and incredulity."

That gentleman smiled and shook his head.

"It is a desperate chance," continued Entrefort, "and is a novel case in surgery; but it is the only chance. The fact that the weapon is a stiletto is the important point—a stupid weapon, but a blessing to us now. If the assassin had known more she would have used——"

Upon his employment of the noun "assassin" and the feminine pronoun "she," both Arnold and I started violently, and I cried out to the man to stop.

"Let him proceed," said Arnold, who, by a remarkable effort, had calmed himself.

"Not if the subject is painful," Entrefort said.

"It is not," protested Arnold; "why do you think the blow was struck by a woman?"

"Because, first, no man capable of being an assassin would use so gaudy and valuable a weapon; second, no man would be so stupid as to carry so antiquated and inadequate a thing as a stiletto, when that most murderous and satisfactory of all penetrating and cutting weapons, the bowie-knife, is available. She was a strong woman, too, for it requires a good hand to drive a stiletto to the guard, even though it miss the sternum by a hair's breadth and slip between the ribs, for the muscles here are hard and the intercostal spaces narrow. She was not only a strong woman, but a desperate one also."

"That will do," said Arnold. He beckoned me to bend closer. "You must watch this man; he is too sharp; he is dangerous."

"Then," resumed Entrefort, "I shall tell you what I intend to do. There will undoubtedly be inflammation of the aorta, which, if it persist, will cause a fatal aneurism by a breaking down of the aortal walls; but we hope, with the help of your youth and health, to check it.

"Another serious difficulty is this: With every inhalation, the entire thorax (or bony structure of the chest) considerably expands. The aorta remains stationary. You will see, therefore, that as your aorta and your breast are now held in rigid relation to each other by the stiletto, the chest, with every inhalation, pulls the aorta forward out of place about half an inch. I am certain that it is doing this, because there is no indication of an escape of arterial blood into the thoracic cavity; in other words, the mouths of the two aortal wounds have seized upon the blade with a firm hold and thus prevent it from slipping in and out. This is a very fortunate occurrence, but one which will cause pain for some time. The aorta, you may understand, being made by the stiletto to move with the breathing, pulls the heart backward and forward with every breath you take; but that organ, though now undoubtedly much surprised, will accustom itself to its new condition.

"What I fear most, however, is the formation of a clot around the blade. You see, the presence of the blade in the aorta has already reduced the blood-carrying capacity of that vessel; a clot, therefore, need not be very large to stop up the aorta, and, of course, if that should occur death would ensue. But the clot, if one form, may be dislodged and driven forward, in which event it may lodge in any one of the numerous branches from the aorta and produce results more or less serious, possibly fatal. If, for instance, it should choke either the right or the left carotid, there would ensue atrophy of one side of the brain, and conse-quently paralysis of half the entire body; but it is possible that in time there would come about a secon-dary circulation from the other side of the brain, and thus restore a healthy condition. Or the clot (which, in passing always from larger arteries to smaller, must un-avoidably find one not sufficiently large to carry it, and must lodge somewhere) may either necessitate amputa-tion of one of the four limbs or lodge itself so deep within the body that it cannot be reached with the knife. You are beginning to realize some of the dangers which await you."

Arnold smiled faintly.

"But we shall do our best to prevent the formation of a clot," continued Entrefort; "there are drugs which may be used with effect."

"Are there more dangers?"

"Many more; some of the more serious have not been mentioned. One of these is the probability of the aortal tissues pressing upon the weapon relaxing their hold and allowing the blade to slip. That would let out the blood and cause death. I am uncertain whether the hold is now maintained by the pressure of the tissues or the adhesive quality of the serum which was set free by the puncture. I am convinced, though, that in either event the hold is easily broken and that it may give way at any moment, for it is under several kinds of strains. Every time the heart contracts and crowds the blood into the aorta, the latter expands a little, and then contracts when the pressure is removed. Any unusual exercise or excitement produces stronger and quicker heart-beats, and increases the strain on the adhesion of the aorta to the weapon. A fright, fall, a jump, a blow on the chest—any of these might so jar the heart and aorta as to break the hold."

Entrefort stopped.

"Is that all?" asked Arnold.

"No; but is not that enough?"

"More than enough," said Arnold, with a sudden and dangerous sparkle in his eyes. Before any of us could think, the desperate fellow had seized the handle of the stiletto with both hands in a determined effort to withdraw it and die. I had had no time to order my faculties to the movement of a muscle, when Entrefort, with incredible alertness and swiftness, had Arnold's wrists. Slowly Arnold relaxed his hold.

"There, now!" said Entrefort, soothingly; "that was a careless act and might have broken the adhesion! You'll have to be careful."

Arnold looked at him with a curious combination of expressions.

"Dr. Entrefort," he quietly remarked, "you are the devil."

Bowing profoundly, Entrefort replied: "You do me too great honor;" then he whispered to his patient: "If you do *that*"—with a motion towards the hilt—"I will have *her* hanged for murder."

Arnold started and choked, and a look of horror overspread his face. He withdrew his hands, took one of mine in both of his, threw his arms upon the pillow above his head, and, holding my hand, firmly said to Entrefort,—

"Proceed with your work."

"Come closer, Hippolyte," said Entrefort, "and observe narrowly. Will you kindly assist me, Dr. Rowell?" That gentleman had sat in wondering silence.

Entrefort's hand was quick and sure, and he used the knife with marvellous dexterity. First he made four equidistant incisions outward from the guard and just through the skin. Arnold held his breath and ground his teeth at the first cut, but soon regained command of himself. Each incision was about two inches long. Hippolyte shuddered and turned his head aside. Entrefort, whom nothing escaped, exclaimed,—

"Steady, Hippolyte! Observe!"

Quickly was the skin peeled back to the limit of the incisions. This must have been excruciatingly painful. Arnold groaned, and his hands were moist and cold. Down sank the knife into the flesh from which the skin had been raised, and blood flowed freely; Dr. Rowell handled the sponge. The keen knife worked rapidly. Arnold's marvellous nerve was breaking down. He clutched my hand fiercely; his eyes danced; his mind was weakening. Almost in a moment the flesh had been cut away to the bones, which were now exposed,—two ribs and the sternum. A few quick cuts cleared the weapon between the guard and the ribs.

"To work, Hippolyte—be quick!"

The machinist had evidently been coached before he came. With slender, long-fingered hands, which trembled at first, he selected certain tools with nice precision, made some rapid measurements of the weapon and of the cleared space around it, and began to adjust the parts of a queer little machine. Arnold watched him curiously.

"What——" he began to say; but he ceased; a deeper pallor set on his face, his hands relaxed, and his eyelids fell.

"Thank God!" exclaimed Entrefort; "he has fainted—he can't stop us now. Quick, Hippolyte!"

The machinist attached the queer little machine to the handle of the weapon, seized the stiletto in his left hand, and with his right began a series of sharp, rapid movements backward and forward.

"Hurry, Hippolyte!" urged Entrefort.

"The metal is very hard."

"Is it cutting?"

"I can't see for the blood."

In another moment something snapped. Hippolyte started; he was very nervous. He removed the little machine.

"The metal is very hard," he said; "it breaks the saws."

He adjusted another tiny saw and resumed work. After a little while he picked up the handle of the stiletto and laid it on the table. He had cut it off, leaving the blade inside Arnold's body.

"Good, Hippolyte!" exclaimed Entrefort. In a minute he had closed the bright end of the blade from view by drawing together the skin-flaps and sewing them firmly.

Arnold returned to consciousness and glanced down at his breast. He seemed puzzled. "Where is the weapon?" he asked.

"Here is part of it," answered Entrefort, holding up the handle.

"And the blade——"

"That is an irremovable part of your internal machinery." Arnold was silent. "It had to be cut off," pursued Entrefort, "not only because it would be troublesome and an undesirable ornament, but also because it was advisable to remove every possibility of its withdrawal." Arnold said nothing. "Here is a prescription," said Entrefort; "take the medicine as directed for the next five years without fail."

"What for? I see that it contains muriatic acid."

"If necessary I will explain five years from now."

"If I live."

"If you live."

Arnold drew me down to him and whispered, "Tell her to fly at once; this man may make trouble for her."

Was there ever a more generous fellow?

- - o O o - -

I thought that I recognized a thin, pale, bright face among the passengers who were leaving an Australian steamer which had just arrived at San Francisco.

"Dr. Entrefort!" I cried.

"Ah!" he said, peering up into my face and grasping my hand; "I know you now, but you have changed. You remember that I was called away immediately after I had performed that crazy operation on your friend. I have spent the intervening four years in India, China, Tibet, Siberia, the South Seas, and God knows where not. But wasn't that a most absurd, hare-brained experiment that I tried on your friend! Still, it was all that could have been done. I have dropped all that nonsense long ago. It is better, for more reasons than one, to let them die at once. Poor fellow! he bore it so bravely! Did he suffer much afterwards? How long did he live? A week—perhaps a month?"

"He is alive yet."

"What!" exclaimed Entrefort, startled.

"He is, indeed, and is in this city."

"Incredible!"

"It is true; you shall see him."

"But tell me about him now!" cried the surgeon, his eager eyes glittering with the peculiar light which I had seen in them on the night of the operation. "Has he regularly taken the medicine which I prescribed?"

"He has. Well, the change in him, from what he was before the operation, is shocking. Imagine a young dare-devil of twenty-two, who had no greater fear of danger or death than of a cold, now a cringing, cowering fellow; apparently an old man, nursing his life with pitiful tenderness, fearful that at any moment something may happen to break the hold of his aorta-walls on the stiletto-blade; a confirmed hypochondriac, peevish, melancholic, unhappy in the extreme. He keeps himself confined as closely as possible, avoiding all excitement and exercise, and even reads nothing exciting. The constant danger has worn out the last shred of his manhood and left him a pitiful wreck. Can nothing be done for him?"

"Possibly. But has he consulted no physician?"

"None whatever; he has been afraid that he might learn the worst."

"Let us find him at once. Ah, here comes my wife to meet me! She arrived by the other steamer."

I recognized her immediately and was overcome with astonishment.

"Charming woman," said Entrefort; "you'll like her. We were married three years ago at Bombay. She belongs to a noble Italian family and has travelled a great deal."

He introduced us. To my unspeakable relief she remembered neither my name nor my face. I must have appeared odd to her, but it was impossible for me to be perfectly unconcerned. We went to Arnold's rooms, I with much dread. I left her in the reception-room and took Entrefort within. Arnold was too greatly absorbed in his own troubles to be dangerously excited by meeting Entrefort, whom he greeted with indifferent hospitality.

"But I heard a woman's voice," he said. "It sounds——" He checked himself, and before I could intercept him he had gone to the reception-room; and there he stood face to face with the beautiful adventuress,—none other than Entrefort's wife now,—who, wickedly desperate, had driven a stiletto into Arnold's vitals in a hotel four years before because he had refused to marry her. They recognized each other instantly and both grew pale; but she, quicker witted, recovered her composure at once and advanced towards him with a smile and an extended hand. He stepped back, his face ghastly with fear.

"Oh!" he gasped, "the excitement, the shock,—it has made the blade slip out! The blood is pouring from the opening,—it burns,—I am dying!" and he fell into my arms and instantly expired.

The autopsy revealed the surprising fact that there was no blade in his thorax at all; it had been gradually consumed by the muriatic acid which Entrefort had prescribed for that very purpose, and the perforations in the aorta had closed up gradually with the wasting of the blade and had been perfectly healed for a long time. All his vital organs were sound. My poor friend, once so reckless and brave, had died simply of a childish and groundless fear, and the woman unwittingly had accomplished her revenge.

THE END

Also from Benediction Books ...
Wandering Between Two Worlds: Essays on Faith and Art
Anita Mathias
Benediction Books, 2007
152 pages
ISBN: 0955373700

Available from www.amazon.com, www.amazon.co.uk

In these wide-ranging lyrical essays, Anita Mathias writes, in lush, lovely prose, of her naughty Catholic childhood in Jamshedpur, India; her large, eccentric family in Mangalore, a sea-coast town converted by the Portuguese in the sixteenth century; her rebellion and atheism as a teenager in her Himalayan boarding school, run by German missionary nuns, St. Mary's Convent, Nainital; and her abrupt religious conversion after which she entered Mother Teresa's convent in Calcutta as a novice. Later rich, elegant essays explore the dualities of her life as a writer, mother, and Christian in the United States-- Domesticity and Art, Writing and Prayer, and the experience of being "an alien and stranger" as an immigrant in America, sensing the need for roots.

About the Author

Anita Mathias is the author of *Wandering Between Two Worlds: Essays on Faith and Art.* She has a B.A. and M.A. in English from Somerville College, Oxford University, and an M.A. in Creative Writing from the Ohio State University, USA. Anita won a National Endowment of the Arts fellowship in Creative Nonfiction in 1997. She lives in Oxford, England with her husband, Roy, and her daughters, Zoe and Irene.

Visit Anita at
    http://www.anitamathias.com, and
Anita's blog Dreaming Beneath the Spires at:
    http://theoxfordchristian.blogspot.com, and
Anita's Read Through the Bible blog at:
    http://readthroughthebiblewithanita.blogspot.com/

The Church That Had Too Much
Anita Mathias
Benediction Books, 2010
52 pages
ISBN: 9781849026567

Available from www.amazon.com, www.amazon.co.uk

The Church That Had Too Much was very well-intentioned. She wanted to love God, she wanted to love people, but she was both hampered by her muchness and the abundance of her possessions, and beset by ambition, power struggles and snobbery. Read about the surprising way The Church That Had Too Much began to resolve her problems in this deceptively simple and enchanting fable.

About the Author

Anita Mathias is the author of *Wandering Between Two Worlds: Essays on Faith and Art.* She has a B.A. and M.A. in English from Somerville College, Oxford University, and an M.A. in Creative Writing from the Ohio State University, USA. Anita won a National Endowment of the Arts fellowship in Creative Nonfiction in 1997. She lives in Oxford, England with her husband, Roy, and her daughters, Zoe and Irene.

Visit Anita at
   http://www.anitamathias.com, and
Anita's blog Dreaming Beneath the Spires at:
   http://theoxfordchristian.blogspot.com, and
Anita's Read Through the Bible blog at:
   http://readthroughthebiblewithanita.blogspot.com/

www.ingramcontent.com/pod-product-compliance
Lightning Source LLC
Chambersburg PA
CBHW020143150626
46552CB00021B/1601